WE TAKE ME APART

Molly Gaudry

Ampersand Books
www.ampersand-books.com

ISBN: 978-0-9887328-8-9
First Ampersand Books edition

Cover design by Matthew Revert

Typesetting by Robert Hamilton

The publisher would like to thank Enterprise Car Rental, Café Envie, Google Maps, Lhasa Apsos, Haveneses, New Orleans, I-75, and The Musician.

Additional praise for We Take Me Apart

"In Molly Gaudry's novella in verse, *We Take Me Apart*, the ordinary becomes mythical, what may be autobiographical becomes fable, and simple lines or sentences ring with ominous music. Even the empty space between the lines seems to resonate with invisible narrative. A stunning debut."

—Richard Garcia, author of *The Persistence of Objects*

"Entwining the trance that is childhood around the hallucination that constitutes adulthood, Molly Gaudry's *We Take Me Apart* is a bewitching and carefully barbed tale. A cross between silence and a fairy tale, Gaudry's Beckettian narrative sews bright bits to near-faint whispers, slowly swaddling us in quiet and darkness."

—Brian Evenson, author of *Fugue State*

"Molly Gaudry's *We Take Me Apart* works "thread into lace" . . . especially vivid in this book-length work is the mother's entrance and exit, where the ragged lines swell and turn sonnet-like with love."

—Terese Svoboda, author of *Weapons Grade*

"Molly Gaudry's *We Take Me Apart* is a dazzleflage of a book. The stuttering disrupted language of this cubist concoction disappears before your ears, sinks into your eyes. This aggressive dress camouflage reweaves Gertrude Stein's rewoven grammar of worsted silk-screened gabardine into a fully ripped patois-ed pattern of stunning wonder."

—Michael Martone, author of *Michael Martone*

long ago

in a different version

it was not a glass slipper but a glass dress

it was not beautiful

it was not flowing like a stream

it did not have a train wider than an acre

in this version everyone could see everything

nothing was left to the imagination

due to the drought

all the people in the town

children too

used their spades to uproot the vegetable gardens

day after day

after day

the day finally came when all they could do was look
into the cloudiness and pray

disgraced

for why else would the gray lining of their clear sky
withhold unless it had been decided that the only
useful thing was for them to suffer

there was not so much as a cabbage leaf that year

cold came to be known as night

heaviness was no longer a worry

the town turned to violence

a rich man's cook was discovered making sauce in
the heart of his house

as everyone knows that food does not smell until it
boils

until it sweats

the people still there

who had not yet gone away

their bellies round with malnutrition

tongues useless calluses

detected that woman's sauce

came for her with a knife

the first ingredient they added was her toe

cut at a neat incline

they called it butter

they added her bottom half

called it custard

her top half

they called tea

when she cried they heard only the whistles of their
stomachs filled with her

they raised their glasses

toasted

this is the story Mother told to get me to behave

tucked into my bedding

I once asked BUT WHAT ABOUT THE GIRL IN THE GLASS DRESS and Mother's answer was JUST COUNT YOUR LUCKY STARS YOU'RE SAFE IN BED AND NOT A COOK FOR A RICH MAN

the way he made her feel

the way he looked at her

she left nothing to the imagination

because Mother was not supposed to have a child

I made it difficult for her to retain employment

so it was sometimes as if I never existed

I was never taught to read or write

there was always so much else to do

the sewing

tending garden

selling its offerings

the cleaning of our living spaces

which

while small

were not so humble as to be neglected

it was not always work

because there were so few others in our lives we
were starved for attention

so Mother made up a game called flattering

to play I had to pay her a compliment

after which she would say THANK YOU and give me a
thing she had found or been given

the yellow rubber innard of a frog's eye

bloody feathers

a fistful of water

although we were never rich or well-attended

with such playthings I was pleased

springs

when the sky was pink

when all the out of doors were bright blossoms of pink

I would have liked to play

but Mother took odd jobs cleaning

brought me along to learn the game of princess

in my favorite house there were copper pots hanging from the kitchen walls

the kitchen was closed to the woman of the house

the cook had rules

one was children should eat cookies quietly at the table while mothers cleaned

those three spring days the game of princess actually
made sense

but there was still the rest of the season

I had never encountered rudeness but from spring
sprung fine tall ladies with short tempers whose
words I scrubbed away

desperate for them to relieve us of their gazes so we
could return again to our game in which the trials
were dirt

spotlessness

our single goal

summers there were children to play with but their
finery embarrassed me

I had overheard a mother define play clothes as rags

disposable

of no consequence if misplaced

at home rags were not disposable

if misplaced

the consequence was dirt

fall was when children returned to school

I was grateful to escape them

their mockery of my appearance

which Mother said was not so bad

one year when she came home from market
she frowned and said YOU ARE A WOMAN NOW
AND THERE WILL BE NO MORE GAMES, DO YOU
UNDERSTAND

as there was only one correct answer I said it

that night instead of dinner she said SIT BETWEEN
MY KNEES and when I did she withdrew from her
purse several red leaves that she wove into my hair

she said YOU ARE A QUEEN, MY DEAR AND THIS IS
YOUR CROWN, HAVE PRIDE

I smiled so that she could not see

she reached for something

placed it in my lap

it was a book

I did not know how to use it until she said GO ON,
OPEN IT and all over those pages were photographs
of the world in black and white and many shades of
grain

in the weeks following my crown fell apart until at
last there was only a single red leaf

which I placed between the pages of my favorite
photograph

I did not know it but the photograph was of America

the Statue of Liberty

I did not know that one day many years later I would
stand inside the Statue of Liberty and say HOW
LASTING IS YOUR CROWN, MY DEAR, HAVE PRIDE

winters Mother said TONIGHT IT IS CUTLET every
night

we began each week with a loaf of bread

a knife

she said LET ME CUT THAT FOR YOU and by the end of
the winter I let her cut twelve loaves

how soft it was within those loaves

those crusts that grew harder by the day

I think there is no more perfect place to be than in a kitchen

the kind of kitchen our great-grandmothers knew

something like a cellar with a packed dirt floor

a large stone fireplace with a big black cast iron kettle suspended above rising flames

there are rabbits skinned

hanging on the wall beside root vegetables wrapped with twine

also hanging on the wall

outside the wind is fierce but warm

soft

dim inside

only the sound of knitting needles clicking

making tender objects out of wool

a vagueness in the air

but in this kitchen there is no such thing as blind

it is happy here

like a wedding with so many guests standing is the
only option

were I not so negative I would bargain it all to end
up in a kitchen like this

but only a fool bargains on faith

and today it is elbow macaroni

which means it is Saturday

noon on the nose

tonight it is soup

cake the texture of carpet

which means it is six o'clock

Thursday

what I want is to taste with deliberation the way
a quiet meadow becomes dimmer after a wetting
around the edges

but today it is asparagus

Friday

five forty-five

I have no need for a timepiece

I was once a slender woman

but weight is meaningless

or might as well be

I have not felt slender in years

I have grown large and it makes me worry I no
longer know myself the way I knew myself when I
was a girl and Mother would mark my height on the
doorframe with a pencil in one hand and a butter
knife in her other and it is not difficult to recall the
feel of that cold metal on my scalp and how I was
quite afraid she might cut me if I was careless so
I never moved an inch but held my breath until it
sometimes hurt until she said ALL RIGHT THEN, TAKE
A LOOK and I would dip under her arm and turn and
grin like a chimpanzee with an orange wedge in my
mouth and watch as she marked the mark with my
initials and the month and year

if someone were to mark me now on either side she
would probably need both sides of the doorframe
because it has been a long time since I left this room
and when I entered I was a slender woman and all
they do is feed a person here and this is how I have
come to mark the passing of time

tonight it is mashed potatoes

this morning it is a puffed pastry

this morning it is two fried eggs

today it is a small loaf of bread

tonight it is cow

all of it enough to make a person want to hurl her
plate

but here they are not of the shattering kind

the woman down the hall is wailing again

if only I were allowed to stitch the wall

we might not have to bear her every morning

if there is a how to describe the what I feel then
a dead-red-roses-filled and fingerprint-smudged
carafe on the center of a table in the center of a room
in the center of a house in a place called before the
stitching years

where I have long collected dust

forgotten skin

fallen hair

sloughed cells that nowhere rise with the entrance of
a body

yours

perhaps

in an otherwise empty room that has been

will be

when you one day make your way to the center of
this house

the center of this room

you will reach and lift that carafe to expose a small
clean perfect circle

you will be holding me

this is something you left me wanting when you left

or maybe not a carafe but sugar in a lidded bowl on
a cluttered counter in a busy shop in a place called
now

here is where the well-known people meet and hug

kiss each other's wind-red cheeks when they come
go

the well-known people

they scoop me with a tiny spoon

you are the spoon in me dividing me

the bowl beneath me supporting me

the lid above me that shuts out the light

they scatter me onto the counter where I spread into
a pretty pattern

they stir me into steaming cups until I am gone

something else entirely

less sweet

hot

wet

like the morning after the last rain when drenched
daffodils turned disfigured bells toward dawn

petals torn atop a dead fat robin's breast

the ravaged lawn

the night before I had requested something sweet

Mother melted cocoa for that midnight feast

rain pounded the sill

lightning lit our sweat

the well-known people

when they lick the tips of their fingers

press into me on the counter

I will this way be lifted into the air

brought to winter lips

in warm moist mouths dissolve

in a different version it was not a pea but a cocoa
bean

you came to us in the night

soaked in cold

trembling with fatigue

Mother brought you inside where the last of our
candles were burning

prepared for you a bed of many mattresses

in the morning she asked how you had slept

you nodded

I was the one who did the beds

knew you had not slept on those mattresses

had slept on the floor

why

I had never seen a being beautiful as you

who

in passing my cocoa-bean test

brought me great inspiration

the dresses I fashioned from that point forward were
winged creations made from the excesses of water
on hand

each drop sewn one on top of the next so that the
texture was rippling as a pond beneath the moon

the dresses took on the buoyancy of flotation devices

hung in the air around us as I made them

I saw you reach up to touch the hem of the highest
one

when it burst

your hand frozen in the air

you were as wet as the night of your arrival

the children who were to wear those dresses did
not cause them to burst but went away like small
butterflies

one day you indicated by the look on your face that
you had never seen such wearing

after many months

when Mother was away

cleaning homes because it was spring again

you said HOW WOULD YOU LIKE TO GO AWAY FROM
HERE AND TRAVEL THE WORLD WITH ME MAKING
THESE DRESSES and I said I DID NOT KNOW YOU
COULD SPEAK and you said DON'T BE STUPID, OF
COURSE I CAN SPEAK, BUT I HAVE BEEN IN MOURNING
and I said WHAT IS MOURNING and you said
SUFFERING and I said WHAT IS SUFFERING and you
said IMAGINE THERE WERE FOOD IN THIS HOUSE AND
NOT JUST COCOA BEANS BUT SO MUCH FOOD YOU
COULD NOT EAT IT ALL and I said DON'T BE STUPID
and you said THAT WOULD BE THE OPPOSITE OF
SUFFERING and I did not understand but said I SEE

when Mother came home I told her we were leaving
in the morning and she said I CAN'T FORCE YOU TO
STAY and TELL ME WHAT YOU WOULD LIKE

because I knew that all she had was cocoa I said MAY
I HAVE COCOA PLEASE

rain sill lightning sweat

in the morning

petals dead breast lawn

we were gone

in a different version it was not a pistachio nut but a
whaling ship

I had never seen snows but I had heard

dreamed

imagined great pillows of them

warm as a tongue

imagine my surprise when on our journey from
Mother's home to yours you took me on a boat from
which we looked for whales

the only boat I had ever touched was paper

folded by Mother's hands

two twigs tucked in as representations of her

me

you were furious with our captain but I was
delighted

the white

the great cut-shaped mounds were wondrous as
anything I had ever seen

chunks like chocolate

I could have eaten them

I was so happy

happier still when the waves pounded all sides of the
boat and below deck the crash of our bodies woke us

happiest when at last we disembarked

it was raining

it was light

it was fresh

when I remember you that is what I remember

it was raining

it was light

it was fresh

it was fall

it was wet red leaves stuck in clumps to the bottoms
of my canvas sneakers

your rubber galoshes

we shared a menthol cigarette from the freezer

walked hand in hand to the corner store for butter
for pancakes beneath a bright yellow umbrella the
morning after our midnight arrival to your home

you took me in your arms and said WELCOME HOME
and it was all of it delicious

we were open mouths on mouths

hands on inner thighs

fingers spreading toward action

fingers spreading like rhubarb in the garden

we were on the porch attached to the kitchen and I
turned my head into the night and saw the rhubarb
poking through the soil and I felt like the soil and
your tongue felt like the rhubarb and your tongue
felt like the so-slow melting or shaving of the ice on
the mountain and its edges broken into song and
snow that settled as a soil blanket tucked wet and
warm and it was only your tongue between us then
and in my throat I felt we were two lakes meeting for

the first time at the open mouth of a river and you
were no longer stern and unfamiliar but consuming
and radiant and I felt consumed and I felt radiant

beneath our bodies

a loose plank that sounded like the click of two
spoons in a creaky drawer sliding open

I felt beneath you like you were the drawer and I was
the spoon

I felt beneath you like you were a spoon and I was an
egg

ready to hatch

tonight it is pea soup contained in a dinner-roll bowl

which means it will be that time of year again when
the leaves turn the colors of flames

a single red leaf

a Japanese Maple especially

was worth more to me than a dozen red roses' petals
scattered on my bed with pink candles all around

which you thought was so original

so romantic

maybe it was romantic

even if it was not original

it was a violet land the shape of a crescent the shape of a halved heart

had I been smarter or paid more attention

I would have seen it coming

your evening obsession on so many canvases

your orange period

you brought boxes of small animals' bones

left them all over the house

when I asked why you said I HAVE BEEN TOO LONG IN THIS PRISON and I said ALL YOU DO IS HURT A PERSON and you said I'M WORKING, CAN'T YOU SEE, GO PLAY HURT SOMEWHERE ELSE

that was when I began shaving the dog

it was something to do to get your attention

but you did not notice

we were hardly seen that summer

dog and I

we were fools

believed in the possibility of your taking interest in us again but when you did it was not to open up but to neglect

I have twice been accused of exaggerating

the first time you were wrong

it was a ritual of mine to wake early

stay in bed an extra moment with my eyes closed to
better hear the air between your parted lips

listen for the first bird

wait until it finished its morning song

enjoy its morning song with my eyes still closed

after the song slip from beneath our sheet

reach for my robe hanging from the post

cinch it above my hips

tread barefoot to the kitchen to stand before the sink

to slide that red-checkered curtain along the brass
rod

to face the day

tie the sash

to watch the lightening of the light blue sky

I did this every morning

often found myself wishing the window was a
postage stamp

the kitchen an envelope inside a carrier's bag

the bedroom I did not wish to be anything but what
it was

your bedroom

with you in it

asleep

unaware

I said this to you once but how I said it was I'M
LEAVING and you accused me of exaggerating and
said DON'T BE STUPID, YOU HAVE NOWHERE TO GO

you were still up

sitting at the table after a long night who knows where

without turning I said YOU'RE RIGHT, YOU LOOK LIKE YOU COULD USE A REST, GO UP TO BED, I'LL STILL BE HERE WHEN YOU COME BACK DOWN and I was

but not really

someone had told us to try a pet because the shared caring for another could work wonders

I would have liked a cat

to have called it mine

to have rubbed its nose with my nose

but you were a dog person

I think now that if we had gotten a cat instead maybe it would have killed the bats in the attic

those bats

they destroyed us

all because of the hole in your roof

I had said IT WILL NEED FIXING and you said IT ALL NEEDS FIXING and I said YOU ARE EXASPERATING and you said NOT HALF AS MUCH AS YOU and I said

MAYBE YOU SHOULD GO AWAY AGAIN and you said
IT'S NOT A MATTER OF SHOULD, HONEY, BUT WHEN
and I felt sick

the air between us was a thick glare

the time it took for me to move from the sink to the
table was the audible tick of my bare feet on the
boards

mustard was thrown

in the time it took for me to move from the table
to the living room the jar's shards stuck in Dijon
splatters on your painting above the mantel

a blue flower at the base of mountains that I said
looked like a cow

you hit me with your fist that came open at my
mouth

we ruined the furniture that night

I flushed your cigarettes

which was the final straw

in the morning you were gone

I hardly felt the loss of you because it took so much
effort to clean the house

to climb to the attic

to trap the bats

they made me feel as if I had been bitten all over but I regarded them as toys

they were my friends

I played with them

stretched their wings to just beyond capacity

gently wrenched their necks

applied pins to their red eyes before at last I threw them out

set them free into the night

I wanted to exchange places

to be the elegant one who dwindled elsewhere
during the day

to come home to a hot plate

I reached into my sewing bag

found what I was looking for

the necessity of that sharpness

my only resource

obsession

what followed was a mission

I sold everything to a museum

over two hundred originals of the dresses I had
made over the years

whose replicas had made us rich

put all the money in a purse

lobbed it from the window

after

I locked the window

touched the carafe on the table

bent to smell the red roses from our anniversary

then slipped away

beneath a stone pillar I waited for a train to take
me to the country where I would spend two seasons
eating only food I had harvested or killed

someone had told us it was a lover's dream

a haven

a step away from modern life

a way to rekindle

so I went

without you

every morning it was fresh sausages

pig intestines I had cleaned

stuffed with salted ground organs

blood

fat

herbs from the garden

when I left I stood in a field

watched the wind make tall yellow grasses dance
with great black cattle

watched how calm the cattle became

either from the grasses' hypnotic motions or the
sideways grinding of their jaws

it had been too easy

I had made it too easy for you

all I could think was how an attractive person's
charm weakens a doubtful person

how

if I went missing

as was my hope

there was no one anymore who would know to order
a search

I heard a girl scream once

it was the most terrible sound

came from beyond a crescent shadow cast on my
chest by a stone many hundred feet above in a land
hued violet

that was the beginning

what followed was the hairs on my arms raised like a
boar's bristles

my skin wrinkled the texture of a pigskin

the girl was so far away

I could not get to her in time

her scream was like the de-threading of a withered
celery left too long in the cold

terror

I have since thought

is to watch tiny frozen crystals spark then melt in the
air with each destructive pull of strand

or watching cream curdle

or butterflies erupt from the open mouth of an oyster

buoyant

the smell of the lambs after I slaughtered them

to endure it I imagined red rose petals spilling from
their open throats

cascading to the ground

scattering

rather than the gush

the flow

the splatter trickling away

it was a way to re-associate those red roses in that
carafe on the table

those red rose petals on our bed with pink candles
on our anniversary

red roses red roses red roses

why never just a simple red leaf

goddamn you

but that was always the way with you

was it any surprise that after those open throats I
returned to sewing

eventually to making lace

many years later to the making of needle lace that is
white like the white of an eye or the white of a small
animal's skull that resembles a desert rock carved
round by wind

gratitude is a cousin to the squeezing of a heart

think of our long summers and how we roamed
those groves and brought back over the years how
many baskets of citruses we halved and squeezed
until their juices flowed

ran down our chins

when you left I gave up citrus

returned to the task of sewing for I could not bear
the taking of a knife to cut a thing in two

to milk it like the tearing of a leaf along its veins
until white beads emerge

could not bear to bleed it like a cow or a deer

the idea of again binding two or more parts to make
a whole thing

to put together stitch by stitch

became a way to remind that there are things in this
world for which I could be grateful

which is not to say that my heart did not feel
strained

or that what remained was not pulp

a great many things are strong

thread

for instance

which can be snapped in two with a quick pull

can also be wound into binding that cannot be
broken

when I think of Mother now I think how strong she
was

like thread

how she never snapped

how it was her practice to bind and combine

if we had only a single sausage but a wealth of apples
and zucchini then the zucchini became a fleet of

boats and their passengers cubed apples mingling
with the sausage cut into parts
how she liked to wear flowers in her hair

one of my favorite memories is the image of her
sitting on the ground beneath the falling cherry
blossoms

her back toward me

caught in a ray of light

her head on the crook of her arm resting on a green
chair

she was asleep but her fingers were still linked

she had been praying

which is something I had never known her to do

when I was very young a neighbor offered to take
me to church because Sunday was family day in the
home of Mother's rich employer and there was much
to be done in that elegant house

but Mother said I WILL NOT HAVE MY DAUGHTER
EXPOSED TO LYING and she gave the woman a red
rose from the garden for her trouble

when I asked WHAT IS CHURCH she said words I did
not understand and I said WHAT IS FOOL and she
said WOULD YOU LIKE TO PLAY A GAME and I said YES

and she said THE GAME IS CALLED LITTLE WOMEN
and I said HOW DO YOU PLAY LITTLE WOMEN and
she said LIKE THIS and caught me in her arms and
twirled us about until the skirt of my dress opened
wide and became the widening of the rest of the
afternoon

tonight it is boiled peanuts

which means the circus is in town

summer

is there such a thing as a long summer

a summer is a summer

a day only so long until the day is done

a season only as long as a season

but I understand the sentiments of a long summer

which are that it will be a long pleasant summer in
rocking Adirondack chairs on wraparound porches
so old the boards are warped and need repair but not
this summer maybe next because dog is swimming
fetching in the sparkling pond and beyond the
backyard thicket of dark greens and mossy browns
a secret clubhouse in the highest thickest oak and
back at the house the windows open and ceiling fans
twirling and on the porch mint leaves saturated and
fragrant in sweating glass pitchers of peach iced tea
while beneath the fading sun two green-eyed lovers
lighting sparklers and running through the night
to jar fireflies and turn cartwheels and stain green

bare knees and later beneath the brightening moon
fanning themselves and unblousing button tops and
kicking off their shoes and leaning back in their twin
rockers with sighs like loveliness borne into the cool
dark night

or that summer has been too long and an unbearable
hotness in an empty home and every day the
vacuum's hum and by dusk a layer of grime on oily
face beaded upper lip running mascara and damp
underarms and then the trip to market for groceries
and hot bodies all around and upon coming home
there is the stove and a hot meal to make for one
and then hot water for the dishes that need washing
in the sink before which a person stands and says
SOAP, I FORGOT SOAP, I KNEW I WAS FORGETTING
SOMETHING and then her single sigh on its descent
into the heartbreak of hell

for some time during the stitching years I worked for
a small circus

dog was taught to sing

the children loved him

fed him boiled peanuts from a small green tin

it was a good time for hope

the period of our greatest determination

it was easy to escape the point

which was that you had left

it was easy because we were always on the go

though I never slept so well as when I worked for the
circus

there were even curtains for privacy around my cot

I crossed off so many pages of that book Mother had
given me

pleased to see the world

in a different version it was not a beast in a castle but an elephant in a tent

I was allowed to touch her because her headdress needed an alteration I could not do unless she was wearing it

I placed my hand against her trunk

her brown lashes long as streamers

she winked

how grateful I am to have had the chance to touch that elephant with the beginnings of an elephant inside her

which was why her headdress needed loosening

because her neck had gotten fat

but everyone at the circus loved her all the more for it

one of my many employers during the stitching years
liked to give me her old clothes

like a soft red cloak that was at the time several sizes
too large but fits me now

so I wear it

people here call me the woman in the blue coat
whose greatest virtue is that she is patient

the wearing has that quality

but it is not a coat

it is not blue

it is a cloak

it is red

I do not understand but when I wear it I feel wealthy
because my employer was a wealthy woman

hired a battalion of seamstresses to build her an
armory of dresses that could be worn until she wore
them out

another of the seamstresses

Charlotte

who was one of my favorites for she was kind

eventually quit with the intention of starting her own
business

on the sly I sent her an occasional dress of sewn
flower parts

the wealthy woman did not like to wear a dress made
from flower parts and said FLOWERS ARE TOO FINE
TO BE WORN AND DIE BESIDES, AND I LIKE TO WEAR
A THING THAT LASTS LONGER THAN A MOMENT AND
HAS A PERMANENCE but really it had more to do with
what she considered wasted time because our time
was her time and valuable in her opinion and she did
not like for it to be wasted on dresses that could only
be worn once

it was a fine excuse to be able to make those dresses
for Charlotte

who believed in the impermanence of objects

the lasting unlastingness of things meant to be
appreciated in a moment

their moment

and what is a moment but a fragment of an
experience and what is an experience but a fragment
of understanding and what is understanding but a
fragment of recognition and what is recognition but
the thing by which we can know and be known and I
was so known for my dresses made from flower parts
that eventually I had to quit my employer and join
with Charlotte and when I did my employer gave me
her red cloak

which I had made several years before

but she did not want any reminder of me around

I have had it ever since

I began to produce several dresses a week and in the
making of them not a single flower part was left out
because every part has a function and I believed then
in the function of things and how things could work
and become the becoming of another

or at the very least a whole thing that was more than
just its parts

for we are more than our parts

we are all of us more than our parts

we are

all of us

more than our parts

the women who wore my dresses knew this

as the parts of their dresses were

petals

that attract and can be scented

I liked to think these women wore their dresses in order to attract

I liked to think of these women strutting city streets and herds of children following

stigmas

covered in sticky so pollen adheres

I liked to think of these women strolling through fields of wildflowers and all the wildflowers' pollen lifting into the air and attaching like metal shavings to a magnet

styles

raise stigmas from ovaries in order to decrease pollen contamination

I liked to think these women thought they were on the cusp of style

I liked to think of these women sitting crossed-ankled on park benches thinking of their ovaries

I liked to think of these women thinking of how to decrease the contamination of their ovaries

ovaries

protect ovules and become fruit upon fertilization

I liked to think of these women growing larger with
the growths of grapes and cherries and apples inside
them

anything but citruses

of course

for I had given up citruses

which was new to me then and because it was new to
me it was strange and it is strange to think of how I
hated citruses so passionately for I do not hate them
so much now

ovules

that upon fertilization become seeds

like sequins I sewed those ovules to the hems of
those women's dresses and I liked to think of them
shining and glittering as they undressed before the
watching eyes of lovers

receptacles

join flowers to stalks and sometimes become part of
the fruit after fertilization

with the receptacles I sewed buttons so that those dresses would not come undone and leave those women bare without their wanting to be

stalks

support flowers and with them I made seams and stays

nectaries

are where nectar is held and with them I made hidden pockets because every woman should have a place to hide her personals

sepals

protect flowers while the flowers develop from buds

I liked to think of these women protected by their dresses as they felt themselves developing into finer women

filaments

are the stalks of anthers and anthers contain pollen sacs and I like to think now of these women in the moments of their undressing

fragmentary

ripe for fertilization

in a different version it was not a spindle and
uninterrupted sleep but what seemed like a hundred
years of uninterrupted starvation

and it was not straw into gold but thread into lace

if only tears could have served as currency because
all I had to eat in those days were crusts of cucumber
sandwiches at the tea house

a woman there had taken pity on me

it was a fine system she ran

dog and I had been idle many months

it could not have been much worse for us

the woman said YOU NEED A PLAN, DO YOU HAVE ANY
SKILLS and I said I CAN SEW AND HE CAN SING

it was rock bottom by then and my appearance was
laughable but not amusing

if there were cracks I had slipped through them

thanks to the tea house woman

a slow change

dog and I gradually filled up

during our time there

dog provided the entertainment

someone

the very best man I had ever met

eventually said SO THIS IS MUSIC, IS IT and meant it as a compliment

he had filled dog's tin cup so many times it lost its green sheen

I knew we would have to move along but that was a holy time

a healing place

after much preparation dog and I left

but in the meantime the woman had taught me a skill

a new use for thread

so while dog earned his keep outside the tea house
doors

I

shut up in the tea house woman's attic

made her a wedding dress entirely of lace

which she wore in the ceremony beside that very
best man I had ever met

the tea house woman also had a father

a grand old guy

Sam

I had never known men but Sam took me as his
guest

it was the only time I ever wore a dress I had made

I knew there would be many people at the wedding
and between the tea house woman's dress and mine
there could be commissions

the women came in a burst after the cake had been
served

during the dancing they formed rows of one long
elegant neck after another

craning to see the seamstress

as they approached they gave me their cards so that I could call on them in their bed chambers for private fittings

I asked how they had enjoyed the cake

which Sam had made as a gift from oranges and cream

although there was a spoon at my place I could not eat Sam's cake

for each glorious candied orange peel curl tasted as salt upon a sore and on a day as fine as that I would be no licker of unforgotten wounds

but when the last of the women left to dance I pressed my finger into the tablecloth that elsewhere was stained with salad dressing and lifted a crumb to my lips and Sam said SOMETHING TO DRINK and I said PERHAPS A COCOA and I felt inside me the pull of an orange skin from its flesh and the pressure of something unnameable

she caught cold in the chest so called me home and
I went to her to care for her the way she had cared
for me and after a while I began to call her Susan
because I could not call her Mother because Mother
had been black cherries in a bowl and Susan had
become chewed up and pit-spit out and Mother had
been days and Susan was seconds and Mother had
been a massage that eased the soreness of a sprain
away and Susan was the beating of fists and the
bruising of an orange into a plum and Mother had
been a small white bird and Susan was the bones of
the bird fractured like glass that cannot be mended
and Mother had been pepper and Susan was the
mistake that ruins a meal and causes the chef to
throw in the towel and Mother had been news
and Susan was the ash of the remains of crumpled
newsprint and Mother had been a mass

a force

and Susan was sparse

after a particularly bad storm I went outside

brought in all the flowers whose heads hung at
crooked angles

mended their broken necks

it took all night

in the morning I was exhausted

but that was the most beautiful bouquet I have ever
seen

it cheered Mother up

there was not a red rose in it

she liked to call me her little goat because I would
eat whatever she put before me

I would have eaten anything she gave me because
trust is lovely and if you cannot trust your mother
then who

even though she sometimes said TONIGHT IT IS
CHICKEN but really it was rhubarb roots that caused
us to shed pounds

at least we were eating

when I think of Mother now she is cooking in the kitchen

reaching into glass jars

pinching spices with her fingers

I remember how she crushed each pinch between her palms to release its aroma

how it was always a lengthy deliberation

the ruthless choice of one ingredient over another

I remember how kind she was and how everyone always said how loving and kind she was and what a kind and capable woman she always was and it was true and they were right and even though she never had a wedding she always wore white

which made me think she was a nurse before I knew any better because I knew nurses wore white but she was not a nurse

she was a cook

but also a woman of most domestic trades

though she had not been for many years

she was sick

when she spoke her words were a flurried rush from
the shallow space mistaken for her throat

scratched

papered

I begged her not to speak and learned the actions of
her bidding

did them because I could not bear to hear her voice

which in the past had been the bursting of winter
into the green of spring but had become a memory
in the middle of her bed in which she rested not like
vegetables in a salad but vegetables in canned soup

the last thing she said was that she had sold the
house

that the walls needed painted red

I have not seen a red since the stitching years

when I was as a torn wing in wind without direction
of my own

what I would give to see a red again

a berry breaking in the beak of a lone male cardinal
in a bare stark winter forest of black trees lit by
yellow sun

a tulip black and yellow at its center with a ladybug
asleep inside

skin withering wrinkled on fallen apples black seeds
yellow flesh in an orchard glistening with rain

jaunty velvet bows on wreaths on doors of red-brick
homes with smoke choo-chooing from chimneys
and shadows candle-flickering beyond those frosted
panes

the leather leash you clipped to dog's matching collar
before taking him for a romp through the citrus
groves and the rubber galoshes that kept your feet
dry in rain sleet snow and in the summer the way
we tethered him to our picnic table painted peeling
red and covered with a red-and-white checkered
tablecloth thin and tearing beneath red plastic
plates heaped to the hilt with fried chicken parts and
mustard potato salad with chopped hard eggs and
parsley sprigs and green olives with red pimento
hearts for garnish

fingernail polish

on my two big toes

a sequin

discovered in our dryer lint

cloth-bound books in secondhand stores that smell
of cats and old soap and other things like stop signs
the kids graffiti and brake lights on a highway on
a night of purple with stars of white and canvas
sneakers and disposable stirrers and women's moth-
shaped mouths that open wide and wider until their
laughter takes flight and soars and hand-crocheted
caps mittens scarves from leftover yarn and paper
valentines in February that come all the way from
somewhere to the others here by mail and even the
stripes like a candy cane on the American flag that
ripple on stamps on envelopes enfolding paper-doily
cards and I used to love to touch a stamp because the

sender's red tongue had been there however briefly
yet thoroughly but now stamps are stickers and do
you remember making valentines at school and the
melting of cinnamon candies in marshmallow treats
cut into hearts

so many reds

so I sometimes turn to face my window to feel the
breeze if it is open

and the imagining of shapes and colors waiting
beyond the window's glass to greet me is fireworks
spectacular if only one does not become distracted
by the sounds from the television and the people
who dwell there laughing and talking as if they are
the only ones who matter and it seems their friends
and families and lovers allow them to believe this
but in real life this is not often the case

is it

and what is sight anyway but the way by which we
forget our other senses

during the stitching years I would have liked to
have given up all sharp objects but scissors were a
necessary tool for ending thread

fixing ragged fabric edges

if someone were to give me scissors now I would not
know what to do other than perhaps glide the wide
open mouth of them cleanly through the air

which cannot be hurt

it is a curious thing

my not knowing how to handle a tool that I for so
many years quite deftly handled

another curious thing is the word poison preceded
by the word merciful

in a different version it was not three beautiful
maidens but Mother and you and me and in this
version

as in all versions

happiness was her hoped for ever after

then I came along and in this version happiness was
her hoped for ever after for me

but then you came along and in this version
happiness was my hoped for ever after for us

but then you left and in this version happiness was
my hoped for ever after for you

then Mother died and there was only me

happiness

I realized

was a game called temptation that Mother had never
taught me

this is what she taught me

that our house could crumble all around us but we
should say we should all be so grateful as to have a
house to call our own and if an orange were all we
had to eat for a week she would offer it and say SAVE
ME THE PEELS FOR WE WILL HAVE MARMALADE NEXT WEEK
and HOW DOES THAT SOUND

she was the button with which I fastened myself
to the wild world when all were wide open greens
and golfing beneath leisure-blue skies and we were
playing her make-believe game of ducking when she
said FORE to dodge the plaster dropping from our
walls

she was never disappointed and this is what I
appreciate most when I think about her now

which is better than thinking of the scattering
of her remains and how I shut the doors after
the scattering of her remains and wallowed and
remembered how every once in a great blue while
she had saved enough to say TONIGHT IT IS TURKEY
WITH CELERY STUFFING or TODAY IT IS VEGETABLE
SOUP FOR LUNCH or TONIGHT IT IS A ROAST WITH
BOILED POTATOES AND APPLE PIE FOR DESSERT

so it is a cheese sandwich

is it

it is confusing

this is the first cheese sandwich I have had here

is there a new cook in the house

is there a clock in the house

I do not know what day it is or if it is night or
afternoon

the first time Mother made cheese sandwiches we
ate them beneath cherry blossoms that showered us
like confetti at a parade and because the weather was
so wonderful that spring we came to call the space
between the canopy of the cherry blossoms and the
ground beneath our rumps our dining room

in our regular dining room Mother liked to say DO NOT SPEAK UNTIL YOU ARE SPOKEN TO and she rarely spoke to me and so I did not speak

but in our beneath-the-cherry-blossoms dining room she became a great cultivator of conversation and I quite often felt as if we were two women in a garden in a famous painting sitting as we were beneath a parasol of petals protecting us from the sun

someone here has messed her sheets and no one has
bothered to clean her and I am sorry but I blame
you even though I never blamed you for a thing and
I know now this is where I went wrong in the first
place and did you know I dreamed about you many
years after our parting and thought in that dream
how age is the great mellower for you were reclined
on the sofa and looked uncomfortable but you did
not complain

see how the years had changed you

you were wearing a straw hat and dark eyeglasses

I thought how silly you looked

recalled how you did not believe in adornments

which always made the point of what I did for a
living impossible to defend

imagine my surprise when those many years later I
dreamed you thus accessorized

if I could have had it my way I would have walloped
you good but then I noticed when you got up you
were stumbling as you walked from what had been
our living room to the water closet

the width of the doorframe around you made
you look so small I did not knock the way I had
journeyed so far to do

did not knock the way I had planned for so many
years

to tell you

finally

just where you could go

I woke instead

left you be

left us

after so many years

at long last

be

nobody speaks to me here but this is okay because
words are often a blaming chain of carelessness

disappointment passes eventually

like now

I feel a calmness coming

like a dark saloon at the end of the night when
during the day it is washed in the color of sky

when I think of Mother now I think of us as little
women wearing white dresses with red ribbons
woven into our hair and our dresses spread as wings
and our ribbons trailing through the air and the
air is a letter and our ribbons are the stripes of the
letter's lines and the lines are the boundaries before
the signing of sincerely

below us people are huddled in an alley and pointing
because our straight flight pattern is a message and
the message is there is nothing to fear

we have come

we are here to take away all hurt

the people are fainting because our coming is the
taking of their terror into custody

their hurt was once the fragile middle of a pearl but
our arrival is the purple shine of the pearl

it is a delicate process of selection but with the intention of missing no one we swoop down and cover them with our bodies and wash them at length with our tears until there is no longer any such thing as complication in their lives

when from them we depart

two trains in opposite directions in the night

they are as a town reborn by the arrival of a depot releasing them from their previous isolation

WHAT I WANT IS TO TASTE WITH DELIBERATION THE
WAY A QUIET MEADOW BECOMES DIMMER AFTER A
WETTING AROUND THE EDGES

I said this not long ago for no reason really except
that by taste with deliberation I meant hope and by
quiet meadow I meant baby and by dimmer I meant
calm and by a wetting I meant pink lips and by
around the edges I meant clamp mother's breast

a revision

then

of what I want

which is to hope the way a baby becomes calm after
pink lips clamp mother's breast

in a different version it was not a poison apple but a
red rose

which Mother placed first in her mouth

one petal at a time

chewed

then passed

her lips on mine

into mine

for it was all she had to give me

that red paste that stained our gums

our tongues

our teeth

as by then I was too old for nursing

too young for solid food

even now when I eat there is a cutting feeling of joy
but sodden in so many shadows that I have come to
be known here as the woman in the blue coat whose
greatest virtue is that she is patient because she has
been waiting a very long time

for what

I cannot say

I feel as though I live within a cinched brown bag

a paper lung

something happened after Mother died

it involved scissors

I had shut the doors

everyone was gone

I was alone

I removed the scissors from my sewing bag

I held the handles in my hands

pointed their points toward my eyes

and then the blood through which I saw the walls at
last were red

is there an undertaker in the house

someone should send for him

the woman down the hall did not wail today

listen

if nothing else

I am at least a woman who has known and loved the company of a lamp in a dark and empty room

Molly Gaudry is also the author of a short fiction collection, "Lost July," available in the 3-author volume *Frequencies* from YesYes Books, and a nonfiction collection, "Wild Thing," available from The Cupboard. She is a core faculty member of the Yale Writer's Conference and the creative director of The Lit Pub.

CPSIA information can be obtained at www.ICGtesting.com
Printed in the USA
LVOW13s2152220614

391190LV00003B/170/P